Passing The Puck

A hockey adventure

David Jacobs

ACKNOWLEDGMENTS

This short story was written in just a few short days while vacationing on the French River with my wife, daughters and my wife`s parents. The story and characters came so easily because of the hundreds of great memories I have growing up in Toronto, Ontario, Canada, playing hockey in the streets in the summer and on the ice in the winter. I hope you enjoy the story and appreciate this great team sport just a little bit more.

For Dad, for letting us play the sport we loved.

For JJ, Holder, Hatchig, Peter, Neil and the Baroness boys, who made it possible to enjoy the best team sport.

And for Mikey, for watching my back when you weren`t checking me, and when you were.

CHAPTER 1

Sweat ran off the damp blond hair sticking out from under Sam's toque and dripped onto the ice. His hands gripped his stick backwards, holding the tip of the blade just shy of the invisible face off dot. As he felt the motion of Grandpa's hand dropping the puck everything began to move in slow motion, the puck waffling slightly in mid-air as it floated downward.

It was getting dark again, another game pushed into overtime. Sam's legs were burning and with the sun gone down he should have been cold, but he wasn't, his skin drenched in hot sweat with more pouring out. Two old farm vehicles parked behind either net were idling, their dim head lights casting a faint glow and long shadows across the ice.

Just before the puck hit the ice, Sam swept it out of mid-air and back to Marty, his left defense. As Marty zoomed the puck cross ice to his partner Skip, Sam spun away from the other team's centre and looped over to the right side of the rink. Skip waited until the opposing winger started skating towards him, then zipped the puck back to Marty who had floated back five feet. Marty quickly redirected the puck past the forechecking winger and up ice to Jamie, his left winger.

Billy, their right winger, was skating up the middle as Jamie's hard pass hit the tape mid-stride and Billy split the defense. The defense chased Billy hard, their sticks snipping at his feet and legs trying to distract him.

The goalie sensed that Billy would not have time to wind up his big shot, so he stayed close to his net to protect against the deke. Billy kept the puck in front of him as he focused on keeping his skates moving to stay ahead of his pursuers. The deke was not Billy's forte but he only needed the goalie to bite on the deke. Billy looked up just in time to stick handle to the left around the poke check, but couldn't flip it over the goalie because he was going too fast.

Planning on this Billy kept skating, cupped the puck in his blade, and leaned in tight as he boomeranged around the back of the net. Instead of going for the wrap around, he fed the puck right to Sam in the high slot who was streaking in behind the defense. Sam's wrister hit the mesh in the top of the net.

"We won!" Billy yelled as he crashed into Sam.

They fell to the ice and Jamie, Skip and Marty piled on top. A few long seconds later their goalie Meat joined the pile. Sam laughed at his teammates' hollering until he heard a cracking sound close to his ear.

"Get off!" he yelled frantically. "Get off! The ice is breaking!"

CHAPTER 2

The fragrant aromas of cumin, tumeric and cilantro filled the kitchen. "Dinner smells delicious mother."

"Thank you Nirha. Please go tell your father and brother it is time for dinner."

Nirha found her older brother Suneel in his bedroom listening to the radio. "Time for dinner. What are you listening to?"

"Nothing," replied Suneel as he turned off the radio and walked past Nirha down the hall towards the stairs. Nirha walked over to the radio and turned it on.

"Thank you for your calls tonight," said the announcer. "This ends our Buds talk program. Please join us again next time." Nirha had a puzzled look on her face as she left the room. Why would her brother be listening to a radio show about buds?

"Suneel please pass the Naan bread," asked his father. "Mother your butter chicken is even better than my mother's!"

"I should hope so," his wife chided.

"Son, do you agree this is a glorious meal your mother

prepared for us?" asked Suneel's father.

"Yes, father it is," Suneel replied. "Uh…"

"No 'uh' son, do you have something to say?"

"I was wondering if we could have mac and cheese one night?" Suneel asked sheepishly.

"Do not be ridiculous Suneel," his mother replied sharply. "Where did you get such an idea?"

"Mikey in my grade 7 class said it's his favourite meal mom," grumbled Suneel.

"That's enough Suneel," interrupted his father. "And, you will address your mother as 'mother,' not 'mom.' Now, let's change the subject. Mother, were you out at the market today?"

"It's called a 'grocery store' dad," said Suneel under his breath.

Ignoring his son, his father continued, "Mother did you see anything interesting?"

"The 'market'," Suneel's mother said, adding emphasis and looking directly at Suneel with raised eyebrows, daring him to correct her, "was uneventful. But all I hear everywhere I go is talk of the Toronto professional hockey team."

"That's because this year, 1993, is their year to win it all!" explained Suneel.

"Hockey is a barbaric game," said his mother disdainfully. "And the fact that so many Canadians love it makes me wonder about our new country."

Suneel's mouth dropped in shock. "No mom, it's the best game!" he replied enthusiastically.

"First," his father said sternly, "you will address your mother as 'mother' or you'll leave the table; second, the fact that they misspell leaves with a F clearly shows the game is created by uneducated barbarians; and third, there will be no arguing this point Suneel, cricket is the greatest game on earth. Now, go change, you have cricket practice in thirty minutes."

Ninety five minutes later Suneel and his father were driving home from the indoor cricket practice. "You practiced well son."

"Thanks dad." Suneel winced as he heard the words leave his mouth. "I mean, father" he said, quickly correcting himself.

His father gave him a sideways glance while driving. Their family had only been in Canada for seven months and his son was adapting the fastest. His accent was quickly fading and he was picking up the local slang quite rapidly. He wondered if he and his wife were being too strict about his language and other cultural adaptations.

Suneel interrupted his father's thoughts. "You are right Da.., er Father. Cricket is a great game; even indoor practice was fun today."

His father sensed there was more to come and stayed silent.

"And I like wearing your number four," continued Suneel. "Did you know one of the greatest pro hockey players also wore #4?"

"I did not know that," answered his father, annoyed with the direction this conversation was headed.

"I was thinking about my birthday."

His father sighed. Oh no, here it comes.

"For my birthday I'm asking for a hockey net, stick and balls, so I can play road hockey with my friends."

"Road hockey?" repeated his father.

A surge of hope welled up inside Suneel as he turned his deep brown eyes towards his father, "Yes, it's hockey outside, without skates."

"Son, I understand a lot of boys at your school like hockey and talk about the pro league. And I know you want to fit in, in our new country."

Suneel's face changed to a glum look of unhappiness. Oh no, here it comes.

"But your mother and I do not want to see you get hurt playing that violent game," finished his father.

"But dad!" whined Suneel.

"No 'but' Suneel. And, you will address me as Father."

A few weeks later on his birthday Suneel got a shiny new bike.

CHAPTER 3

After a few unseasonably warm weeks March break arrived in grand style, with no snow and warm, sunny skies. Suneel counted the hours to Saturday afternoon. After cricket practice he jumped on his bike and raced to the edge of their subdivision, where two of his friends were waiting. He was disappointed they couldn't play ball hockey on such a mild day but hoped they'd find something fun to do together.

Petre Ardelean, better known as Pete, had arrived first. He was from Romania, his Mom and Dad were scientists who left as soon as the iron curtain fell. They had science experiments for him to do over March break, but did not yet realize that the holiday had started. Distracted by their own inventions and side experiments, it would probably be Tuesday before they realized Pete was on vacation. Pete had a rusty old BMX, was dressed in a faded plaid shirt that was untucked over dark grey shorts, mis-matched socks and old runners. His orange hair was ruffled but his blue eyes sparkled clear behind his glasses; glasses that partially covered his freckled cheeks. Pete didn't care much what he looked like and he was as sharp as a tack.

David Jeremiah Eckstein, better known as DJ by his friends, was waiting with Pete. His family had moved from Israel two years ago. His father was a family doctor and DJ had two younger brothers. DJ's dad loved tennis and he wore a bright blue t-shirt that said, 'Camp David' in Hebrew on the front, with a picture of a tennis racket on the back. DJ had a big head of curly brown hair and light brown eyes.

DJ waved as Suneel rode up. "Hey Neel," which is what his school friends called him.

Pete looked at Suneel's clothing and smiled. "No time to change out of your fancy cricket uniform?"

"No better than you two," laughed Neel. "In your experiment clothes and tennis gear." Pete and DJ looked at their clothes and laughed too.

Gus, Tony and Mikey rode up.

Gus's real name was Guilio Fotopoulos and Tony's was Antonio Costa. Gus was Greek and Tony was Italian. Their families were neighbours. Gus' parents were teachers and Tony's were in real estate. Their parents were fiercely loyal to their cultures and argued about pretty much everything, except soccer. Well, that too. Both families loved soccer and their three sets of boys always ended up on the same teams. Gus and Tony still had on their red soccer jerseys from indoor practice earlier in the day. They both had dark hair and black eyes but that's where the similarities ended. Gus was short with thick wavy hair and a round face while Tony was tall with straight hair, a long thin face and a square jaw.

Mikey's real name was Michael Smith and his family was from Saskatchewan. His parents grew up in rural farming towns and had moved east last summer for his dad's banking career. Mikey was tough, but fair. He had blue eyes and sandy blond hair; he was medium height with a strong stocky frame. None of the school bullies dared mess with any of Mikey's friends.

Suneel and his five friends were a real hodge-podge mix. What united them was they all moved into the new Brampton sub-division, Alfalfa Meadows, within weeks of each other last summer. Before summer ended they met a few times in the neighbourhood and on the first day of school they found themselves in the same grade 7 class at Corn Acres Public School. By the second recess the pack was formed.

"Welcome to March break boys!" said Tony as he skidded to a stop.

"We thought it might end before you showed up," said Pete dryly.

DJ laughed.

"Ha ha," said Gus in reply. "Seriously, what should we do today?"

"I'd say ball hockey, but you sissies don't play," said Mikey with a snicker.

"You know we want to," replied Neel.

Mikey finished Neel's sentence with a whiney voice, "But your mamas won't let you."

"Even if they did," Pete said in cool technical voice, "the community council for Alfalfa meadows voted yesterday to ban street games."

"No way," huffed Gus, who clearly had not heard the news yet. "They can't do that."

"They can and they have," said Pete. "My parents were there and told me at breakfast."

"What will they do if we get caught? They don't have any legal jurisdiction," DJ said matter of factly.

"True," admitted Pete, "but they do control access to the community centre. So they decided that punishment would be restricted family privileges to the new centre."

"That is likely to be an effective deterrent," concluded DJ.

"Listen to these two," laughed Tony, pointing at Pete and DJ. "The scientist and the doctor."

Everyone laughed but Pete and DJ, who both studied their friends stoically.

"Oh well," said Neel. "We weren't planning on playing anyway. Let's race to the old f..."

The word 'field' was drowned out by the sound of spinning tires as five bikes took off, leaving Suneel to catch up.

CHAPTER 4

On the north edge of Alfalfa Meadows sub-division a few unfinished streets lay empty, awaiting phase 2 building. The ground was roughly bull-dozed with sporadic heaps of dirt. The six boys sped across this wasteland, launching off small mounds and splattering wet mud behind them. At the edge of the empty block was a steep, deeply rutted hill that ended with a barbed wire fence, a hill they had named 'death valley'.

Without fear, Mikey and Tony, who were in the lead, rocketed right over the crest; according to their boyish pride, the others had no choice but to follow suit.

Neel was still in the rear and slowed down just a touch before going over. The hill was so steep he felt like he was going to fly right over his handle bars. The bouncing of his wheels through ruts sent vibrations from his toes to his eyeballs. Everything was a blur as he sped down the hill, trying to avoid getting caught in a deep rut that might throw him into a terrific tumble.

Just as he made it to the last stretch, the ground leveled out and Neel braked hard to skid his back tire in a fancy fish tail stop. Mid-skid his back tire hit a wet patch of grass, his bike slipped, he fell on this side, with his bike on top of him, and he slid into DJ and Pete. The other three boys bent over in laughter while the three tried to pry themselves out of the tangled pile of limbs and wheels.

Neel was the last to get up. "Whoops," he offered quietly, as he rubbed his aching limbs.

"Oh your mom's gonna love that!" said Gus pointing to Neels' white cricket shorts. A long green and brown skid mark slashed across the bum.

"What?" replied Neel, "Isn't cricket played on grass?"

"Aren't your practices indoors?" asked Tony.

"Right," sighed Neel.

They all chuckled.

Pete dusted himself off and looked around. "Guys," he said, getting their attention and pointing to the field on the other side of the barbed wire fence. "When did that corn grow in the field?"

They all turned and looked in stunned silence at a field full of mature corn stalks. They walked along the fence a few hundred feet until they got to the break in the fence that they always passed through.

"We were here last week after school and it was an empty field," said Mikey. "It was deserted. Hadn't been plowed in years.

Now there's corn almost five feet tall? It would take months to grow that much." No one questioned Mikey's statement and not because he was the toughest in the group. Mikey grew up playing in farm fields in Saskatchewan. The other five were all city kids.

"Yes, and for most of the last two months it has been below freezing and the ground was frozen and covered with snow," added Pete.

Tony, always practical, said, "Well the rows are too tight to ride through."

"Let's park our bikes a few rows in," said Gus.

DJ looked unsure. "And then what?"

"Let's go exploring!" said Neel.

CHAPTER 5

"Stop!" Gus called out. "I feel like we're lost. All I can see is corn in every direction."

"Maybe we should try to retrace our footprints," suggested DJ.

"The ground is too hard," observed Pete.

Mikey spoke up from the front of the line. "We're okay guys. The sun has been on our right the whole time. I've been keeping track of it. Let's keep going, the field's gotta end soon."

They all agreed and followed Mikey in single file.

A little further and the field took a turn upward and they started a long, steady incline.

As Mikey crested the hill he stopped. "Guys shhh." Everyone paused. "The corn ends just over the hill and there's an old barn. Since we're trespassing I suggest we go stealth." Mikey raised his hand with the thumb up. The five returned the signal.

It was a big wooden barn. A foundation of large stones and mortar supported the two and a half storey structure. Windows at ground level belonged to a basement. Based on the smell, there were barn animals living down there. They crept quietly around the corner to one of the short sides of the barn and found a ramp leading down to a set of basement doors. The one door was slightly ajar and some hay was lightly scattered on the dirt ramp.

Whoever left it ajar was probably nearby. Mikey pointed to the open door and put his finger to his lips to keep quiet. They crept around the next corner and down the long wall of the barn, keeping away from the basement windows.

Tony looked up at the three windows high above his head on the second storey, he half expected to see someone looking down at them, but saw nothing.

Mikey stopped at the corner of the barn and the boys all pressed against the side behind him. It was eerily quiet.

"HONK! HONK! HONK!"

The boys hearts almost jumped out of their chests as a goose bolted around the corner chasing a chicken. They all started laughing until Pete realized how loud they were and elbowed Gus. "Shhh," he said. The shushing was repeated up the line until quiet was restored.

Recomposed, Mikey took a look around the corner. His eyes scanned a dirt road with worn tire tracks on either side of a grass median. Then, across a line of trees, he could see the old farm house in the distance. No movement there. Except for the buzz of insects and chirping from birds nearby everything was quiet. He gave the all clear thumb up signal and motioned for them to follow him.

A dirt ramp led up to a wide sliding wood door, three to four feet above the basement. The gravel crunched under the boys' sneakers as they tip-toped up the slope. The door was open about 10 inches.

Neel was the first to peek inside. He turned back to his friends, smiling and said, "You won't believe it," then he squeezed sideways into the barn.

CHAPTER 6

They stood just inside the barn door, letting their eyes adjust to the dimly lit interior. Narrow shafts of light from the cracks in the walls and larger shafts of light from the second story windows criss-crossed each other in the open space in front of them. Fine dust particles hung suspended in the air; air which smelled of dried wood, hay and animals. The second storey and rafters were partially full of hay bales. The wide wooden floor planks were swept clean. At either end of the barn was an old iron hockey net.

Eyes aglow, the boys looked at each other.

"Awesome, eh?" said Neel aloud.

"Indeed," said DJ.

"Look! Sticks!" said Tony walking over to a row of six sticks lined up against the wall. The wooden sticks had flat blades and looked old. Instead of brand names on the sticks, like Koho or Sherwood, each one had a boy's name burned into the wood: Sam, Skip, Billy, Marty, Jamie and on the goalie stick, Meat.

In an old creaky trunk beside the sticks they found balls and goalie equipment.

"Cool," said Gus, picking up the goalie equipment, which consisted of a baseball glove, catcher's mask, chest pad, girdle and a blocker made from wood with holes drilled in it, attached to a leather glove. He also found homemade goalie pads made from thick denim and stuffed with wool. Gus got Tony's help tying the pads to his legs using the old shoe laces strung through the pads.

Within minutes Gus was in net and getting peppered with shots from the other five. Gus kicked out his left foot and deflected a low shot from Tony.

"Beautiful toe save by the Cat," Mikey said, imitating the announcer's voice that called the pro hockey games.

"Watch this wrist shot," said Neel as he leaned hard on the stick, snapping a shot into the top corner past Gus's glove.

"Top shelf where the peanut butter is kept," laughed Tony.

"Very accurate shooting," remarked Pete.

"Oh yeah, try that again, cricket boy," taunted Gus.

"No over here," called DJ from the other side. "Killer slap shot coming!"

Gus got a piece of it with his blocker and the ball caromed to the far corner. As DJ trotted over to retrieve the ball, the others continued shooting on Gus, calling out their other favourite pro hockey players' names.

DJ ran his ball up the barn, stick handling around the

supporting beams. He streaked in on the empty net at the far end, deked past an imaginary goalie and back handed the ball into the net.

"Toronto beats Montreal for the cup!" DJ cheered.

"Fine deke there, young man," said an adult voice.

Startled, DJ spun around to see the silhouette of a farmer standing in the door they had come through. As he stepped into the barn DJ got a better look at him. He had on a worn set of coveralls over a dark work shirt that was pressed and buttoned up to the second last button. On his feet he wore heavy boots caked with wet and dry dirt. He had a thick neck and chest, his face was grizzled and deeply tanned; under his faded cap, white hair crowned his ears.

He pointed a thick hand towards the empty net. "Fine deke," he repeated.

"Thank you sir," DJ replied trying to mask his apprehensive thoughts. The wooden planks creaked as the old farmer started across the floor.

Gus spotted him, stepped out of the net and raised his glove. "Guys, hold up."

They all turned to face the farmer. He stopped about ten feet from them. They each fidgeted a bit, their shoulders hanging low, embarrassed to be caught uninvited in his barn. He stared each one of them in the eyes, one at a time. They saw sternness, honesty and kindness in his eyes. One by one, each boy dropped his gaze from the farmer's unblinking stare. They knew what question was coming.

"Who let you in?" came the rhetorical question.

Just then a black and white border-collie mix came trotting into the barn and stood at the farmer's side. It sniffed at the boys and growled low. "Easy boy," soothed the farmer and the dog sat down at his side. Eyeing their strange mix of clothing and cultures the farmer asked, "Where you boys from?"

"We live in Alfalfa Meadows," answered Neel.

The farmer gave a puzzled look when he heard Neel's Indian accent. "'Alfafa Meadows' you say?" asked the farmer slowly.

Neel nodded and replied, "Yes, in the homes on the other side of your corn field."

The farmer rubbed his chin a bit perplexed. He was about to ask who gave someone permission to build homes in his alfalfa field, but he was pulling weeds there only yesterday and there were no houses then. Something inside whispered to take a different line of questioning. He pointed his finger and moving it side to side, asked, "So you boys like to play hockey, eh?"

Sensing that they were not getting in trouble, at least not yet, the boys breathed a sigh of relief.

"Yes sir," answered Pete in his thick Romanian accent.

The farmer raised his eyebrows as he turned to look at Pete.

Another strange accent.

"We want to play in the pro hockey league someday," added Neel.

"You boys must be new 'round here," observed the farmer.

Nods all around.

The farmer had watched them a few minutes from the door way. They had natural talent and more importantly, they had passion for the game and for playing with each other. "You boys ever played on a team together?" he asked.

"No."

"Never."

"Not yet."

"Is there a league you play in?" he queried further.

"Not really," said Mikey.

"Is that a yes or no?" the farmer asked directly.

An idea came to Mikey and he stepped forward confidently. The farmer raised his eyebrows, impressed with Mikey's leadership. "There's a ball hockey tournament in one week, this Saturday in the community centre. We're entering ourselves as a team."

The other boys looked at Mikey in disbelief.

The farmer eyed them curiously.

Mikey continued, "But some of us are new to the game and we've never played together as a team, so we kind of need a coach, and somewhere to practice."

His friends' jaws dropped.

The farmer's eyes narrowed and he rubbed the grey stubble on his as he surveyed the motley crew before him.

"I have five rules," he said.

CHAPTER 7

"Rule #1, no cursing.

Rule #2, no cheating.

Rule #3, play as a team.

Rule #4, give 100%, hustle, hustle, hustle.

Rule #5, follow your coach and captain.

Who's in?" the farmer finished.

The farmer put his own hockey stick in front of him as he asked the question. Where his stick came from none of the boys knew; they hadn't noticed it before now. The farmer's stick had 'COACH' burned on the shaft. The boys stepped forward and put the blades of their sticks on the farmer's forming a circle around the stick blades.

"I'm in," said Neel happily.

"Me too," the others added.

"Well then, call me COACH BING!" said the farmer, sounding much younger than he did a few moments earlier.

Coach Bing ran them through a long series of drills. First they did wind sprints and then ran the sides of the barn (sticks only), weaving in and out of the support beams. They did push-ups, sit ups, squats and lunges. After 60 minutes they were exhausted and thirsty.

"Pump's right outside," said Coach pointing to the barn door. The boys looked at each other confused but wandered outside in silence.

"That must be it," said Mikey pointing to a black iron pump with a large cup beside it, "I remember one from an old farm back home."

"How do you use it?" asked Tony, looking very thirsty.

Pete was examining the apparatus. "I hypothesize," he began, "that you raise this wooden lever up and down."

That was enough for Tony, who quickly started pumping the handle. It was stiff at first. Just as it began loosening up, water gushed out of the nozzle. DJ quickly put the large cup underneath the nozzle and took a deep drink, "Ah!" he said with satisfaction as Gus took the cup out of his hand.

Meanwhile, Neel stuck his head right under the nozzle soaking his head and then cupped his hands to drink. Tony gave a few more pumps and bumped Neel aside to do the same. Within minutes the boys were wet from the waist up and laughing.

"Save some for the animals," laughed Coach from the barn door.

"Time for scrimmage?" asked Gus.

"No scrimmaging yet. You boys need conditioning and basic training first."

"Ah, come on Coach," complained Tony.

"Remember rule #5 guys," said Mikey. "Follow the Coach."

Coach smiled. "You boys go have dinner. Next practice is 10am Monday. Bring a bag lunch. Enjoy tomorrow with your families." And with that, Coach walked down the ramp and headed towards the corner of the barn.

"Thanks Coach Bing!"

"G'night Coach Bing!"

Coach raised his hand in acknowledgement as he disappeared around the corner of the barn.

The six boys found their bikes on the far side of the corn field and after swearing each other to total secrecy, they promised to meet at death valley at 9:45am Monday and then rode home.

CHAPTER 8

Sunday was a long day for Neel as he waited for Monday to arrive. When it finally did he wished it was Sunday again. His body ached all over when he woke up. Every muscle hurt from Saturday's drills.

After breakfast he asked his mom if he had any chores to do before he went for a bike ride with his friends. She eyed him suspiciously then asked him to turn over the soil in the garden. That was harder work than he had banked on, but was careful not to complain when his mother checked up on him.

When he was done he asked, "Mother, may I take some lunch with me? We're planning on biking for the morning and afternoon."

"Okay Suneel. Be careful. And remember who you are." Her last phrase was her favourite. And Neel didn't mind it; it kind of made him feel special.

"Thank you mother, I will."

He gingerly rode his bike across the sub-division and found all five friends waiting at the top of death valley.

"What took you so long?" asked DJ.

"Gardening," replied Neel.

Remembering the pile up from two days ago Pete said, "You go first this time Neel."

Neel pedaled to the front. Oh great, that means I can't go slowly. He pedaled a few times as he crested the top of the hill and then the steep decline did the rest. His bike picked up speed very quickly and continued to go faster and faster. It vibrated and bounced sending shock waves through his already aching body. He couldn't slow down with his friends right behind him. "AAAAHHHHHHH" he shouted, his voice breaking up into rapid audible bounces, "AAHH!" "AAHH!" "AAHH!" "AAHH!" "AAHH!" Everything was a blur as the barbed wire got closer and closer. Finally he hit the bottom and braked hard, skidding to a stop two feet from the flesh tearing fence.

Skid. Skid. Skid. Skid. Skid. His friends arrived behind him.

Like Saturday, they parked their bikes among the corn and made their way to the barn. The barn was empty again so they grabbed the sticks and balls and began shooting on Gus. After about twenty minutes of practicing on Gus they were interrupted.

"All warmed up?" asked Coach as he leaned on his stick. He was dressed exactly as he was on Saturday.

The first sixty minutes of practice were a carbon copy of

Saturday's. After a brief water break the boys came back in and were thrilled to see the balls out. Coach demonstrated a few passing plays with Mikey and then paired the boys off to practice.

Gus, the goalie, was paired with Tony.

"The goalie needs to know how to handle the ball too," said Coach.

After thirty minutes of ball handling Coach taught them two breakout plays which the five boys practiced while Coach worked with Gus. Gus was sure Coach Bing could score at will but instead he picked apart every inch of Gus's body. Gus was ready to beg for relief when Coach stopped.

"It's noon," Coach said to the team. "Very good work this morning boys. You've made great progress. Take an hour lunch," and he left the barn.

The boys took their bagged lunches out to the water pump. Outside it was a warm, sunny day with a light breeze and not a cloud in the sky. The boys were tired and quiet as they ate. Lunch never tasted so good.

CHAPTER 9

"It's one o'clock," said Pete looking at his watch. The boys walked up the ramp, into the barn and stopped in their tracks. At the other end of the barn were three boys, two taking shots on a goalie. None of the six friends had seen anyone enter the barn over lunch. The three boys at the far end of the barn turned to look at the six boys. The goalie wore equipment similar to Gus's. The other two boys had on white t-shirts with suspenders holding up dark shorts, and socks with short leather boots. A long awkward moment was interrupted by the dog which ran up to one of the three boys and licked his hands.

Coach Bing came walking in a moment later. "Good afternoon boys." Pointing to each of the nine boys in turn he said, "Mikey, Neel, Pete, DJ, Tony and Gus, this is Skip, Marty and Meat."

Coach turned to the six boys. "Mikey you're centre, Neel left wing, Pete right wing, DJ left defense and Tony right defense. Mikey, you're the team captain. You lead your team in a quick warm up and then you'll scrimmage against these three."

The six boys smiled at each other. Six against three, they were going to win no problem.

Coach watched them closely.

Mikey and his teammates grabbed the sticks they had been using from the side wall. DJ noticed his stick had the name Skip on it. Tony noticed his had Marty on his. DJ and Tony looked at the sticks, each other, then across the barn at Skip and Marty who nodded at them. DJ and Tony nodded back. Mikey led his team through wind sprints and then they warmed up Gus.

Coach blew a whistle at centre. The five boys lined up in the standard formation, three forwards, two defense. Mikey faced off against Skip with Marty behind him to the left.

Skip won the draw back to Marty. Pete ran towards Marty who waited and then side stepped Pete in a flash. Neel crossed over from the left side to the right side to challenge Marty. Marty passed the ball to the far right wall where Meat appeared out of nowhere. Mikey ran towards Meat who passed the ball up the wall to Skip who was unchecked with Neel out of position. DJ, on left defense, ran to check Skip but got quickly deked out. Skip ran down the right wall while Marty streaked up the middle to make it a two on one against Tony, the lone defense still in the play. Skip fired a pass under Tony's stick and Marty one-timed it past a sprawling Gus, who had slid across a fraction too late. Skip and Marty casually trotted back to their end and tapped sticks with

Meat.

Coach blew the whistle at centre, "1-0. First team to three goals wins."

"Come on guys," encouraged Gus. "Remember rule #3, play as a team. We've got them out numbered, we can beat them."

Mikey walked to the face off, but before he leaned in he looked at his wingers. "Let's play our positions this shift." They nodded back.

Marty took the face off this time in place of Skip. Marty won the face off and slapped it past Mikey into the far corner to Gus's left. Tony turned and ran to get it. Marty was hot on his heels.

"Man on," warned Gus. Tony flipped the ball up the wall to Neel as they had practiced. Neel threw a blind pass up the middle to where he thought Mikey would be. Skip anticipated the centering pass and raced in, picked off the pass and fired a slap shot from the high slot. The shot was wide and Gus let it go untouched to the wall behind him. Marty was there in a flash to pick up the rebound off the wall and slip it in the net behind Gus, who wasn't tight to the post.

Coach blew the whistle at centre, "2-0."

Mikey motioned for the team to gather around him. "Okay, we're better than this. I'm going to win this next draw and everyone spread out. Find the open space and don't pass unless you have a clear lane."

Coach blew the whistle a second time.

Mikey won the draw and the boys held control of the ball with good passes but could not get a clear shot on Meat.

Skip stood up to a slapshot from Tony and the ball ricocheted off Skip's shin and past Tony. Skip ran in alone on Gus who made a great toe save on a low hard wrister. Gus's teammates cheered and after some hustle and good passing Neel scored their first goal on a rebound.

Coach blew the whistle at centre, "2-1."

A few minutes later Marty ripped a snap shot off the inside of the post to win the game 3-1 for his team.

All nine boys took a break at the water pump.

Gus complimented Marty on his game winner, "Nice snapper."

"Thanks. Nice toe save on Skip. He usually scores on that shot."

"Thanks."

"I think this is your stick," DJ said to Skip.

"That's okay, you use it."

"Thanks."

"Game two," called Coach from the doorway above.

The next game was a hard thirty minute game. Mikey's team won 3-2 with two goals from Neel and the winner from Tony on a wrist shot after he pinched in from the point.

The boys took another water break after game 2.

In game 3 Gus made a dozen strong saves to back his team to a

3-1 win.

The two teams shook hands and put the equipment away.

"10 am tomorrow," said Coach.

CHAPTER 10

The next morning, Tuesday, there were 4 boys waiting in the barn. "Boys this is Billy," Coach said, pointing to the new boy.

"Hey," said Billy.

"Hey," replied the six boys.

After warm-up Coach blew the whistle at centre. "Game 1, first team to 4 wins."

Twelve minutes went by very quickly and Billy completed a hat trick to give his team a decisive 4-1 win. While Billy and his teammates left for a drink Mikey and the boys sat around Gus's net.

"Man, do they move fast," said Tony.

"I never know where they're going, they're always moving and don't seem to play any one position," added DJ.

Coach was standing nearby listening quietly.

"Coach, what can we do better?" asked Mikey.

"When you cut a chicken's head off," Coach started. "It runs around out of control for a few seconds. You're not chickens, so stop running around like them."

"Coach is right," said Mikey. "Everyone play your position."

The next game was a see-saw battle. The score was tied 3-3 for 10 minutes until one of Marty's blasts deflected off Tony's leg, up and over Gus into the top of the net.

As the six boys huddled around Gus, Coach walked over. "That was better. Next game use your defense more in their end to spread them out and put a screen in front of Meat."

The third game was long, with both teams digging deep at both ends. Gus played amazing, stopping three break aways. After Billy tied the game at two a piece Mikey flipped Pete back to defense and brought DJ up to the winger.

Before the draw Mikey winked at DJ. He won the draw and snapped the ball right up the middle. DJ raced after it, his speed caught Skip and Marty by surprise, leaving DJ with a clear path on the goalie. He faked right, then deeked left and back-handed a shot over Meat (just like he had practiced on the empty net on Saturday).

"Nice deke young man," said Coach, winking at DJ.

"Thanks Coach Bing."

A few minutes later Neel scored the fourth and winning goal on a one timer from Pete.

The two teams shook hands and headed for the pump.

Gus was the last one leaving the barn. He turned to Coach. "10 am tomorrow Coach?"

Coach Bing nodded.

The next day was Wednesday. It was cool and the forecast called for rain.

This time the boys were not surprised to find another new boy in the barn with Billy, Skip, Marty and Meat. The six walked right over.

"Let me guess, you're Jamie right?" asked Neel looking down at the name Jamie on the new boy's stick.

Jamie nodded and pointed to Neel's stick, which also had 'Jamie' on it. "I burned that on myself. I heard it works good for you."

"Only a few have gotten past me," said Meat defensively as he puffed out his chest.

"It's a great stick Jamie, thanks for lending it to me," said Neel.

"Ah shucks, don't mention it," replied Jamie with a goofy grin on his face.

WHISTLE.

"Play to 5," Coach announced.

Mikey and his teammates found out in seconds that Jamie was super fast and a great stick handler. But Gus came up big again and kept it scoreless for the first five minutes under a steady assault by Jamie's team.

Pete was becoming a whiz behind the opposing net and scored

the first goal by banking it off Meat's backside when Meat wasn't hugging the post tight enough.

Meat took off his mask and looked like he was going to lose it, but all he muttered under his breath was, "Sugar cane, beets, turnips."

Coach patted Meat on the back. "Pete's got good hands and is creative with the angles. Interesting choice of words by the way."

"Rule #1 Coach, rule #1," replied Meat as he put his mask back on.

Thirty minutes later it was 4-4 when Coach called a water break. As the two teams drank from the pump Mikey asked, "So I guess Sam is going to join us tomorrow?"

Thunder boomed overhead.

Jamie looked sideways at Billy from the corner of his eyes.

"Don't know," said Billy.

Another rumble in the distance.

The game ended on an unusual play. The ball was bouncing in the slot in front of Meat, and Neel swatted it out of the air into the top of the net. DJ clapped Neel on the back, "Just like hitting a cricket ball, right Neel?"

"Pretty much," laughed Neel as his teammates crowded around him rubbing his head to congratulate him.

When Neel arrived home for dinner he noticed his father's car wasn't in the driveway yet. He walked into the kitchen where his mom was preparing dinner. "Where's dad?" he asked.

His mom raised her eyebrows as she replied tersely, "Your father, is at a work function tonight."

"What's a work function?" asked his sister as she walked into the kitchen.

"They are having dinner and then doing an activity," she replied.

"What activity?" asked Neel.

His mother looked at him cooly. She detested lying but she did not want to give her son any false hope. "I'm not sure."

"Are you awake dear?" asked Neel's father as he slipped into bed later that night.

"I was." Neel's mother sat up and turned on the light on the night stand. "How was your dinner?"

Her husband wrinkled his nose. "Dinner was terrible. A cheap Chinese buffet."

"So, that is why you woke me up? To tell me your dinner was terrible?"

His eyes lit up as he smiled. "No. We went to a professional hockey game, do you remember?"

His wife rustled her bed head. Oh no, here it comes.

"I can tell by your expression that you do remember. Well, it was amazing! I was totally shocked. I loved it!"

His wife turned over, switched off the light and went back to sleep.

CHAPTER 11

"Get off! The ice is breaking!" yelled Sam. His teammates finally heard him and started scrambling to get off the pile. Meat rolled to the side as fast as he could.

CRACK went the ice under the pile.

Marty and Skip crawled away on all fours.

CRACK. CRACK.

SPLASH!

The ice broke and Sam went under with Jamie and Billy on top of him. Grandpa arrived at the hole in a flash with a rope. "BILLY! JAMIE! Grab the rope," he yelled. The two grabbed hold and he hauled them out of the ice cold water.

"SAM!" he yelled. "SAM!!!!"

No response and no Sam.

Grandpa pulled on the rope to ensure it was secure. One of the boys from the other team had tied it to the axle of one of the vehicles on the edge of the frozen pond. Grandpa tied it around his waist and jumped in the water. The boys watched in horror as one, two, three seconds passed.

Suddenly Grandpa appeared with his big arm supporting Sam. Marty and Skip pulled him out. Grandpa pulled himself out using the rope, with Meat pulling on the other end as if his life depended on it.

Sam lay motionless on the ice as Grandpa kneeled beside him. Grandpa rolled Sam on his side and gently squeezed his chest. Water came out of Sam's mouth. He rolled Sam back on his back and began the resuscitation methods he had learned in the war.

The frightened boys stood a few feet away and offered silent prayers for Sam as they watched his Grandpa work on him. Finally Sam sputtered and coughed and started breathing on his own. The boys said a silent prayer of thanks.

"We've got to get these three to the hospital. Into the truck, now!" shouted Grandpa.

Skip and Marty helped Jamie and Billy into the truck as Grandpa lay Sam across Meat's arms in the truck. Sam was breathing but still unconscious.

Two days later Sam was still unconscious and Grandpa was still beside his bed.

"Dad," said Sam's father. "Dad, you need to go home and rest."

"I'm not leaving Sam," replied Grandpa.

"Dad it was an accident, nobody is at fault," his son said kindly.

Grandpa's eyes welled up. "I'm not leaving Sam," he repeated.

Two weeks later the same conversation repeated itself in Sam's hospital room. After the same exchange Sam's father added, "The weather has been warm and your field needs plowing and seeding dad."

"Let it go," said Grandpa not taking his eyes off Sam.

"Dad you could lose the farm."

"It'll be fine, son."

"Dad please. Please go home and work your land. I'll stay with Sam."

"Tell Mr. Hodgson my neighbour he can have half the profit if he and his crew will plow and seed it."

"Dad..."

"Half," interrupted Grandpa.

"Okay dad, I'll go talk to him," sighed Sam's father. He leaned over and kissed Sam's forehead before leaving.

CHAPTER 12

Thursday morning was a perfectly clear day. There wasn't a cloud in the sky as the boys rode across the wasteland plot to meet at death valley. A cold crisp wind bit at their faces as they stood at the crest. "Ready?" asked Mikey.

Nods. Thumbs up. Twenty minutes later they were at the barn door.

Inside they found the same five boys as yesterday. No Sam.

Coach Bing walked in behind them and hesitated for a brief moment as he scanned the two teams. Neel, who was standing closest to Coach, thought he saw water in his eyes.

"Let's get warmed up," Coach instructed.

The two teams went through their warm up as one combined group, led by Mikey and Jamie. When they were done Coach blew the whistle at centre.

As the teams lined up it was perfectly quiet for a brief moment, just like the silence before the puck is dropped in a big game. In that brief moment the players, coaches and fans all sense the tension, their anticipation for the ensuing contest fills the air with electricity.

Just as Coach was about to lift his hand to drop the ball the silence was shattered by the sound of the barn door opening. At 10:20am twelve sets of eyes turned to see the silhouette of a boy standing in the doorway.

"Grandpa, can I play?" asked Sam as he stepped into the barn.

The ball dropped out of Grandpa's hand as he walked quickly over to Sam and enveloped him in a huge hug. Tears rolled down Coach's face. "Yes Sam, yes. We've been waiting for you to join us."

Sam's teammates, Jamie, Billy, Skip, Marty and Meat all ran over and hugged him. Mikey, Neel, Pete, DJ, Tony and Gus stood off to the side respectfully. They did not understand what was happening but they knew it was important.

A few minutes later Sam took the face off at centre for his team. A team that was now complete, with five players and a goalie. Coach dropped the ball and Sam won it clean, just as his team won the game, beating Mikey's team 6-0.

In game 2 it was 1-0 for Sam's team when Tony purposely tripped Jamie on a breakaway. Jamie hit the wood floor hard and came up red-faced and angry. His hands had splinters in them and he opened his mouth to say something but closed it again.

"Tony take a seat for five minutes," said Coach, "And think

about rule #2: no cheating. Another infraction and you're out for the game."

When the five minutes was finished and Tony came back into the game it was 4-0 for Sam's team. On the next play the ball was shot deep into the corner to Meat's left. Pete half jogged to get the ball and was beat to it by Marty. The play turned the other way quickly and Sam scored at the other end on Gus, making it 5-0.

Coach called out, "Rule #4 Pete! Give 100%. You plain got out hustled."

"Time out," called Gus.

Coach blew the whistle. "Time out called." He walked over to Mikey's team huddled around Gus.

Gus spoke first, "They're getting too many rebounds guys. I can make the first stop, but I need more help with the rebounds."

"I can play third man in on forward and stay high in the slot, so I can run back to help the defense," suggested Neel.

"Good idea Neel. Do it," directed Mikey.

"Coach," asked Pete. "How can we get more offensive chances?"

"Rule #3, play as a team. And I'll add to that, forget about your position," answered Coach.

DJ spoke up, "But Coach Bing you've been teaching us the positions all week."

"That's right. You have to understand the positions first. But hockey is a game of motion and creativity. On the greatest teams the players know all the positions so well they flow with the game, playing different positions as needed. If you want to beat Sam's team and win the tournament on Saturday, you must truly play as a team."

"We can do that," said Tony "I know we can guys."

Heads nodded.

Suddenly being down by five goals didn't matter anymore.

"One last thought," said Coach quietly and he leaned in. The boys all leaned in attentively. "If the other team doesn't have the ball, they can't score."

The boys all exchanged knowing glances.

On the next play Pete out hustled Marty for a ball in the corner and fed Neel a pass in the high slot who snapped it past Meat.

Coach blew the whistle at centre, "5-1."

Mikey's team scrapped, hustled and sweated their way to three more goals in the next 10 minutes.

Coach blew the whistle at centre, "5-4."

The two teams ran up and down the floor for another fifteen minutes. There were spectacular saves at both ends by Gus and Meat. Neel had the ball down low near Meat's net when he spotted Tony pinching in from the point and fired a pass at him. Sam alertly threw out his stick and tipped the ball, which changed direction and rolled towards centre. Jamie sped past DJ who was caught flat footed. The ball was out ahead of Jamie so Gus came charging out to try to beat him to the ball.

As he raced to the ball Gus realized Jamie would reach it first so he slid out sideways to block as much of the net as possible. Jamie reached the ball in a full run and pulled it out to his left, clear of Gus's feet. A moment later Gus's sliding body crashed into Jamie's feet and legs, sending Jamie's legs up in the air behind him. With his hands still on his stick, his feet in the air and his whole body sailing over Gus, Jamie managed just enough wrist action to shoot the ball towards the net. As he landed on his belly Jamie looked up at the net, and Gus cranked his neck back over his body to see the ball roll into the back of the net.

"Hooray!" cheered Sam's team as they picked Jamie off the ground and exchanged high-fives.

WHISTLE.

"Both teams played a great game," said Coach Bing.

Sam's team began thumping their sticks on the wood floor. Mikey's team reciprocated. The two teams lined up and exchanged the customary "good game" salutation as they shook hands.

"Good luck on Saturday," said Sam to Mikey.

As Mikey's team took a drink at the water pump none of them felt disappointed by the loss. "We played at their level in the second half of the game," said Pete.

"You guys played amazing," said Gus.

"You too Gus," said Tony.

Coach Bing walked up. "Play well on Saturday boys."

"Can we scrimmage again tomorrow?" asked Neel hopefully.

"No. There's nothing left to teach you boys. You're ready for the tournament. Take a rest tomorrow," said Coach.

"You're coming on Saturday, right Coach Bing?" asked DJ.

"We'll see," said Coach with a far away look in his eyes.

"Thanks Coach," said Mikey, standing up and extending his hand to Coach. They shook hands. "Thanks for everything."

The other five boys repeated the sentiment.

"You're welcome boys," replied Coach. "And thank you, thank you boys."

CHAPTER 13

Ring, ring, ring. "Hello?" said Neel's mother.

"Suneel! The phone is for you, it's Petrov."

"Thank you mother, I have it."

"Hello Pete?"

"Neel can you meet at death valley in twenty minutes?"

"What for?"

"I'll tell you there. Call DJ and get him to come too. The others are coming." Pete hung up.

Twenty minutes later the six boys were at the top of the hill. It was 1 pm on Friday.

"So what's the big mystery Pete?" asked Neel.

"Guys you won't believe what I just read in this morning's Brampton Herald," said Pete holding up a cut out news article. Beside the article were two faded black and white pictures, one of Coach Bing and one of Sam. The article title read, Grandson of Coach Bing Passes at Age 61.

Pete read the article out loud.

Yesterday morning at 10:20 a.m. Sam Bing passed away quietly at the Brampton Hospital. Sam was the grandson of the late legendary Team Canada coach, John Bing. Sam had been in a coma for 50 years after a tragic accident on his grandfather's farm. A game of pond hockey turned to tragedy when the ice broke and three boys fell into the frigid water. Coach Bing pulled all three out. The other two boys fully recovered but Sam, Coach Bing's grandson, never regained consciousness. Coach Bing visited his son faithfully for fifteen years before passing away of a heart attack. Sam's passing yesterday closes the final chapter on a story of tragedy and devotion in our community. The Alfalfa Meadows Community Centre will be renamed the John and Sam Bing Community Centre in their memory.

The whistling wind was the only sound as the boys stood in stunned silence. After a few moments Mikey said quietly, "Let's go," and he walked his bike down the steep hill towards the barbed wire fence.

The other boys followed after him in silent procession.

They were not surprised to find a barren field on the other side of the fence. No corn in sight. They rode slowly across the empty field to the barn. The lower windows were boarded up and there was no sound or smell of animals. The barn doors were shut and padlocked. The water pump was rusted, and wouldn't budge.

"Maybe we can see through one of the upper windows,"

suggested Tony pointing up.

Gus and Mikey stood shoulder to shoulder facing the barn wall. Peter climbed up and stood with a foot on Gus's right shoulder and Mikey's left. Then Tony climbed up and stood on Pete's shoulders, then up went DJ and finally Neel climbed up to complete the human ladder.

Neel held tight to the window ledge as he pressed his face against the glass. "Lots of cobwebs," he started. "The rafters are empty. I can see one hockey net and the sticks are lined up against the far wall beside the trunk. That's it. Nothing else."

The human ladder disassembled as the boys climbed down one at a time. "Well what do we do?" asked Gus.

"Ask my parents for a lobotomy?" said Pete dryly.

"Let's go home," said Mikey. "We have a tournament tomorrow." He walked over to the barn and patted the wall. Each of the boys followed in turn, patting the wall as they walked towards home.

CHAPTER 14

The next morning Mikey awoke from a strange dream covered in sweat. All he could remember from the dream was a key hidden under a flower pot.

The family was eating breakfast when Neel finally decided to break the bad news. "Do you know what today is?" he asked.

"Saturday!" shouted his sister.

"Yes it is," said Neel, trying to sound kind to his sister.

He continued, "It's also the floor hockey tournament at the rec centre."

"And why is that important Suneel?" asked his mother.

"Well, I'm on a team with my friends, and I hope you'll come watch us," said Neel as fast as he could.

His mother looked like she was going to boil over but his father put his hand up, stopping her from speaking.

"Suneel, you should have asked us first," said his father.

"I know I should have father, and I'm sorry," said Suneel

humbly.

"Perhaps next time," said his mother.

"Mother please! My friends are depending on me. If I don't play they won't have enough players," pleaded Neel. "Dad, please!"

His dad thought of the hockey game he had watched the other night. His son did not know he had been or that he had enjoyed it so much. He felt a twinge of guilt in his stomach.

"Mother, perhaps we should consider this," said his father very quietly.

She took a long, deliberate breath and exhaled slowly. Am I being too harsh?

Neel held his breath.

"Perhaps," she said finally.

Neel jumped up and came over to hug her and his father, "Thank you mother! Thank you father!"

After breakfast the family walked to the community centre together for the 9 a.m. registration.

"I'm so sorry," said the centre's Director of Recreation to the crowd of children lined up to register. "A pipe burst overnight and the gym is flooded. We'll have to reschedule the tournament."

"Wait," shouted Neel over the disappointed moans of the crowd. "We can have it in the parking lot."

"The council has banned street games," a parent reminded everyone.

"Perhaps we could make an exception," offered one of the parents.

The Director spoke up, "But we cannot use the indoor equipment outside."

Moans of disappointment filled the air from the children.

"Wait!" shouted Mikey. "Give us thirty minutes and we'll have outdoor equipment to play with."

Surprised, the Director paused and then said, "Okay. Let's start the registration then." A cheer went up from the crowd.

Mikey's teammates ran over to him. "Get your bikes and meet me at the barn," said Mikey.

"But it's locked Mikey," said Pete.

"I've got a way in, meet me in 10 minutes at the barn," said Mikey over his shoulder as he ran home to get his bike.

The boys ran home and then raced to the barn, arriving within seconds of each other. Mikey walked over to an old empty flower pot beside the water pump and took a key out from underneath.

"How'd you...?" said DJ

Mikey smiled as he opened the padlock on the door, "That's a little secret between Coach Bing and me."

In addition to the two nets, the boys found ten sticks, two goalie sticks, plenty of balls and two sets of goalie equipment in the trunk; everything they'd need for the tournament. The boys laid the nets flat on the ground and piled the sticks, balls and goalie equipment on top, then each group of three boys carried a net out of the barn on their shoulders.

CHAPTER 15

The crowd gathered outside of the community centre cheered when they saw the boys walking down the sidewalk with the nets on their shoulders. They set up the nets in the empty parking lot and the families gathered around in lawn chairs. It was a gorgeous sunny day and everyone had a great time cheering on the games from the first face off.

The tournament was run as a round robin with each team playing 3 games. The two teams with the best record would square off for the championship game.

Neel had suggested they name their team Bing's Buds, which they did. Bing's Buds won all three games to make it to the championship game, which was set for after lunch.

"Suneel, your mother and I agree we may have prematurely judged hockey as an unsuitable game," said his father at lunch. "You and your friends play very well together as a team."

"Yes," agreed his mother. "I was very pleased with the good sportsmanship. It is not violent like I thought. And it looks like you have been well coached. Who has been teaching you and your friends?"

WHISTLE.

The Director shouted in a loud voice, "The championship game will begin in five minutes. Will the Bing's Buds and the Gibson's Flyers please take the ice now and warm up?"

The crowd laughed at the word 'ice' as the teams ran out on the paved playing surface.

"Gotta go! Wish us luck," said Neel, relieved to have escaped his mother's question.

Five minutes into the game Neel was charging at the right defense when the boy's stick clipped Neel across on the chin on the follow through. A gash opened and started to bleed. Neel dropped his stick and put his hand to his face. The referee blew the whistle and Neel's parents and Dr. Eckstein, DJ's father, ran over.

Dr. Eckstein took a look at it and said soothingly to Suneel's mother, "He will be fine Mrs. Nair. But it looks like it could use a couple of stitches. If you'll let me I do that at my home and have him back in fifteen minutes."

"Will he be okay to finish the game?" asked his mother. Her husband looked at her with a look of shock and admiration.

"Yes I think so," said Mr. Eckstein. "DJ, Seth come with us."

The referee blew the whistle, "Twenty minute injury time out."

Dr. Eckstein had Neel sit on a chair in his garage. "I don't have freezing but if you bite on this piece of leather I think you'll be okay. You'll feel a sharp pain and then pulling on your skin as I thread the needle, okay Neel?"

"I'll be okay Dr. Eckstein," said Neel. "Blood doesn't bother me."

"Okay great," said Dr. Eckstein. "Now Seth," he said to DJ's younger brother, as he handed him a flash light, "you hold this up high so I can see better, okay?"

"Yes Pappa."

Dr. Eckstein began threading the needle and blood oozed out of the gash. The light started to wobble slightly. "Seth hold the light still," said Dr. Eckstein as he continued. The blood was running down Neel's chin and the light was wobbling dramatically now, "Seth! Hold the light …"

Thud.

Dr. Eckstein looked over his shoulder to see Seth passed out on the garage floor. He smiled and turned to DJ, "Put that towel under his head and pick up that light so I can finish this before someone else passes out."

Fifteen minutes later Neel, DJ, Dr. Eckstein and a pale faced Seth arrived back at the community centre.

"Are you okay to play?" asked Neel's father. He nodded yes

and picked up his stick.

As Neel walked out onto the 'rink' the players on both teams slapped their sticks repeatedly against the pavement.

Ten minutes later Pete tipped in a shot from Tony and tied the game 4-4. Whoever scored next would win the championship game. Mikey called a timeout.

"Do you guys remember the last play Coach Bing taught us? He called it the Sam Surprise?"

They all nodded.

"Let's use it now."

They all put their sticks in the middle.

"For Coach!"

"For Sam!"

They lined up for the face off.

Sweat dripped off Mikey's nose onto the pavement. His hands gripped his stick backwards holding the tip of the blade just shy of the invisible face off dot. As he felt the motion of the ref's hand dropping the ball, everything began to move in slow motion, the ball floating downward.

Mikey's legs were burning and his skin was drenched in hot sweat with more pouring out.

Just before the ball hit the pavement Mikey swept it back behind him to DJ, his left defenseman. As DJ zoomed the ball across to his partner Tony, Mikey spun away from the other team's centre and looped over to the right side. Tony waited until the opposing winger started running toward him then zipped the ball back to DJ who had floated back. DJ redirected the ball past the forechecking winger and onto Neel's stick.

Pete, the right winger, was running up the middle as Neel's pass hit the tape mid-stride and he split the defense. The defense chased Pete hard, their sticks snipping at his feet and legs trying to distract him.

The goalie sensed that Pete would not have time to wind up a slap shot, so he stayed close to his net to protect against the deke. Pete kept the ball in front of him as he moved his feet quickly to stay ahead of his pursuers. Deking was not the plan, but he needed the goalie to bite on the deke. Pete looked up just in time to stick handle around the poke check to the left, but he could not flip it over the goalie because he was going too fast.

Pete was planning on this, so he kept his feet moving, cupped the ball in his blade and leaned in tight as he boomeranged around the back of the net. Instead of going for the wrap around, he fed the ball right to Mikey who was streaking in behind the defense. Mikey wristed a shot into the top of the net.

Pete yelled, "We won!" as he crashed into him.

Neel, DJ, Tony and Gus all ran up and piled on as their parents cheered loudly.

CHAPTER 16

A few weeks later the community council rescinded the ban on street games, under pressure from a group of parents led by the parents of the Bing's Buds. The next day the boys were setting up the nets outside Neel's house where the road widened at the end of the cul de sac. They were preparing for a rematch against the Gibson's Flyers.

"Guys I've got bad news," Pete said, holding up a news article.

"Maybe you should stop reading the paper," said Mikey dryly.

The article said that the John Bing farm had been sold by the executor of the Bing estate to the developer who built Alfalfa Meadows. A new sub-division would be going up that summer. The boys were floored.

Two months later the boys stood on the side of the road watching a demolition crew drive their heavy equipment onto Coach Bing's farm. They had enthusiastically painted protest signs but had little hope of stopping the wrecking ball.

The foreman was trying to shoo them away when three vehicles pulled up, an unfamiliar sedan, Mrs. Nair's mini-van and a police car. A woman in a business suit stepped out of the sedan, and to the boys' surprise, all of their parents piled out of the mini-van.

The woman in the suit winked at the boys and said in a thick French Canadian accent, "Nice signs boys."

When she approached the foreman her tone was much different. "Mr. Brown I believe?" He nodded looking perturbed by this interruption. "I am Ms. Ouelette of the historical society of Canada. This farm and all of its buildings and structures has been recognized as an important historical site. Your crew will immediately vacate the site without disturbing anything. I have a document signed by a judge if you wish to see it."

The foreman looked at her, the police car and the boys, who were smiling happily. He grumbled something incomprehensible, then said, "No I don't wish to see it."

He pulled a walkie talkie off his belt, "Tom!"

"Yes boss."

"Get the crew off the site immediately and do not touch anything. We're done here. You got that?"

"Roger that, boss."

Ms. Ouelette turned and gave the boys a wink and the thumbs up signal.

The parents smiled and the boys cheered as loud as they could.

The old farm had been saved, the great game of hockey had been passed from one generation to the next and most importantly, the spirit of sportsmanship and adventure burned bright in the hearts of six young boys.

The End

ABOUT THE AUTHOR

A proud Canadian, David Jacobs lives a blessed life with his soul-mate, their three angel daughters and scruffy dog Casey in friendly Wisconsin, USA.

David grew up in the culturally diverse city of North York (a suburb of Toronto, Canada) and was blessed to enjoy a simple and carefree childhood riding bikes and playing hockey with his brothers and friends.

David can be reached at dg.jacobs@yahoo.ca

MORE BOOKS BY DAVID JACOBS

THE RELUCTANT BEACON   (BOOK 1 OF THE TURLAN TALES)
More great stories coming soon...

www.ingramcontent.com/pod-product-compliance
Lightning Source LLC
Chambersburg PA
CBHW020557130626
46552CB00007B/2930